LADYFINGERS AND LIES

A BELLE HARBOR COZY MYSTERY
(BOOK 14)

SUE HOLLOWELL

D1714111

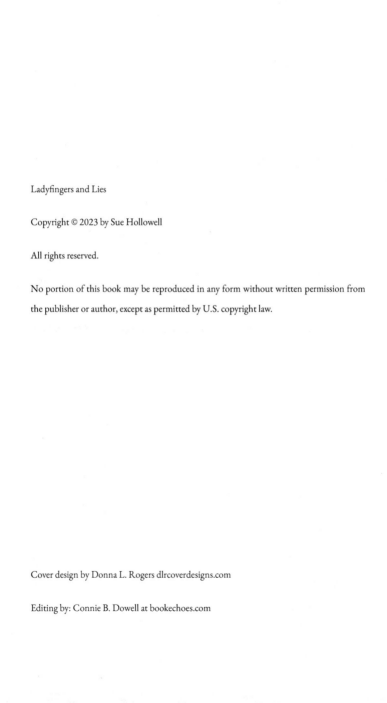

Ladyfingers and Lies

Copyright © 2023 by Sue Hollowell

Cover design by Donna L. Rogers dlrcoverdesigns.com

Editing by: Connie B. Dowell at bookechoes.com

Contents

CHAPTER ONE

"Isn't this just the most wonderful time of the year?" I exclaimed, my excitement bubbling over like an overflowing cupcake tin. Jack, my dear uncle and owner of Checkered Past Antiques, grinned in agreement while adjusting his straw hat to shield his eyes from the sun's glare.

The sun shone brilliantly over the bustling town of Belle Harbor as the annual Parade of Patios commenced. Laughter and chatter filled the air, accompanied by the delightful scent of blooming flowers and freshly cut grass. Each backyard showcased a unique display of creativity and design, making it a feast for the eyes and senses.

"Indeed it is, Tilly! I always look forward to seeing what our neighbors have come up with," he replied, glancing down at the map of participating homes we were following. Linda, Jack's lovely wife and my baking assistant, chimed in, her eyes twinkling with anticipation.

"Last year's displays were simply breathtaking! I can hardly wait to see what everyone has in store for us this year." Her enthusiasm was contagious, and I couldn't help but grin as we eagerly led the parade through the winding streets of our quaint coastal town.

We rounded the corner, and I caught my breath at the sight of Felix's house. A charming coastal cottage nestled amongst lush greenery, with a meticulously maintained garden. The centerpiece of his backyard display was a miniature lighthouse, standing tall and proud amidst swaying beach grass. As we drew closer, I noticed that the tiny structure emitted a magical glow. It cast dancing shadows across the driftwood decorations scattered artfully throughout the space.

"Wow, Felix really outdid himself this year," Unkie mused, scratching his chin in admiration. I nodded vigorously, unable to tear my eyes away from the enchanting scene before us.

"His creativity never ceases to amaze me," Linda added softly, her gaze lingering on the delicate seashells dotting the flower beds. Just then, Felix emerged from his house, beaming as he spotted our awestruck expressions.

"Ahoy there, neighbors!" he called out, waving cheerfully. "Welcome to the Lighthouse Haven! What do you think?"

"Absolutely stunning, Felix!" I gushed, clapping my hands together in delight. "You've truly captured the essence of Belle Harbor."

"Thank you, Tilly!" Felix replied modestly, his cheeks flushing pink with pride. "I wanted to create something that would remind everyone of our beloved town's maritime roots."

"Mission accomplished," Uncle Jack chuckled, giving Felix a friendly pat on the back. "This is definitely going to be a tough act to follow."

Felix grinned, his eyes twinkling with mischief. "Well, I have been known to cause quite the splash at these events," he quipped, eliciting a round of laughter from all of us. "I just hope it's enough to win this year. I think I was in the running last year until Mary came up with that interactive miniature river."

"Alright, folks, let's keep moving!" Uncle Jack announced, clapping his hands together.

I looked at my map. "Why don't we go to Sylvia's house next?"

"Oh, yeah," Linda said. "She's supposed to be the favorite this year."

"I told Hazel we would be there soon. I hear she's got something special planned this year."

"Of course she does," I mused, rolling my eyes playfully. "You know how competitive she gets about the Parade of Patios. She's been trying to outdo herself ever since she took second place last year."

"True," Linda chimed in, her voice lilting with amusement. "Let's hope this year's display doesn't disappoint."

We bade farewell to Felix and continued down the path, anticipation building as we approached Hazel's house. As the town council president, she had a reputation for being fiercely competitive, and her gardens were always a sight to behold.

"Keep your eyes peeled, everyone," Unkie instructed, pulling out the map again. "We should be nearing Hazel's backyard now."

"Is that...a hedge maze?" I asked incredulously, squinting at the towering green walls that loomed before us.

"Looks like it," Linda confirmed, shielding her eyes against the sun as she peered over the top. "Seems like Hazel's really upped her game this year."

"Come on, then. Let's see if we can find our way through," Uncle Jack encouraged, leading the way into the maze.

As we followed Unkie's lead, weaving through the twists and turns of the labyrinthine hedges, I couldn't help but feel a sliver of unease creeping up my spine. Something about the quiet rustle of leaves and the whisper of shadows felt eerily ominous.

"Unkie, are you sure we're going in the right direction?" I questioned hesitantly, glancing back at the winding path behind us.

"Positive," he replied confidently, though I could see beads of sweat beginning to form on his brow. "We're almost there. I can feel it."

"Wait, do you hear that?" Linda asked suddenly, her voice barely above a whisper. "It sounds like...water?"

"Could be a fountain," I suggested, straining my ears to discern the faint sound.

"Only one way to find out," Uncle Jack said resolutely, and we pressed on, the tension mounting with each step we took.

As we turned the last corner, our breaths caught in our throats at the sight of Hazel's backyard masterpiece. The suspense had been worth it, but little did we know what lay beyond this enchanting display.

Just as we were about to step closer and admire Hazel's garden, a piercing scream shattered the tranquil atmosphere. The crash of glass followed the scream, jarring in the otherwise serene setting.

"Good heavens!" Linda exclaimed, her eyes wide with shock. "What on earth was that?"

"Stay here," I instructed, my heart pounding in my chest. I rushed towards the source of the disturbance, adrenaline fueling my movements. Unkie and Linda exchanged concerned glances but stayed put, trusting my instincts.

As I rounded a corner, I came upon a horrifying scene. Hazel stood frozen in place, her hands covering her mouth, her eyes filled with terror.

CHAPTER TWO

On the ground before Hazel lay Heidi, her lifeless body sprawled out amidst shards of broken glass. Her once-vibrant face was now a sickly shade of pale, her eyes vacant and unseeing. What looked to formerly be a dessert trifle was splayed all over Hazel's backyard. Pudding and ladyfinger cookies everywhere.

I gasped, feeling bile rise in my throat. It took every ounce of my willpower not to succumb to the nausea. "Oh, m-my God," I stammered, scarcely believing what I saw. "Hazel. What happened?"

"I-I don't know," she managed between sobs, her voice barely audible. "I just found her like this."

"Did anyone see what happened?" I asked, scanning our surroundings for any witnesses. But there was no one else in sight, only the haunting echo of the scream still ringing in my ears.

"Who could have done such a thing?" Hazel whispered, her face contorted with grief and disbelief.

"Maybe it was an accident," I suggested weakly, though I knew deep down that it was unlikely. There was something sinister about the way Heidi lay there, a small pair of garden shears protruding from her chest.

"An accident?" Hazel scoffed, her tone bitter. "With all the enemies she's made in this town? I doubt it."

"Enemies?" I repeated, my curiosity piqued. Hazel's words hinted at a darker side of the seemingly innocent Heidi, and I couldn't help but wonder what secrets she might have been hiding.

"Never mind," Hazel snapped, her eyes flashing with anger. "It doesn't matter now, does it?"

"Right," I agreed, shaking off my lingering questions. "We need to call the authorities."

I fumbled in my pocket for my phone.

Uncle Jack and Linda arrived as Linda gasped. "Is that...?"

Hazel sniffled, pulling a tissue from her sweater pocket. She nodded. "I don't know what happened."

The chaos that erupted around us was overwhelming. Voices rose in confusion and fear as the formerly celebratory atmosphere of the Parade of Patios took a dark turn. I clutched my phone in my shaking hand, on the brink of dialing the authorities. I spotted Barney, Belle Harbor's police chief, rushing to the front of the parade.

"Barney!" I called out, waving frantically to catch his attention.

He wasted no time pushing through the crowd with a sense of urgency that only heightened the tension in the air. As he approached, I could see the worry etched into his weathered face, his eyes scanning the scene before him.

"By all that's holy…" he muttered under his breath, taking in the sight of Heidi's lifeless body and Hazel's distraught form. "What happened?"

"None of us saw anything," I admitted, feeling helpless in the face of such tragedy. "We heard a scream and then… this."

"Alright, clear out, everyone!" Barney bellowed authoritatively, directing the curious onlookers to leave the immediate area. "Give us some space!"

"Barney!" a familiar voice cried out from the throng of people. It was Florence, Barney's girlfriend and Hazel's sister. Her usually immaculate appearance was slightly disheveled as she hurried towards us in her flouncy skirt.

"Sweetheart, it's not safe!" Barney warned, but Florence paid no mind, throwing her arms around her sister and holding her tightly.

"Who could have done this?" Florence asked tearfully, her snooty exterior crumbling in the face of her sister's distress.

"Let's not jump to conclusions," Barney cautioned, ever the professional. "I'll sort this out, but right now, I need to call in my deputy and secure the scene."

"Of course," Florence nodded, her hands shaking as she wiped away her tears. "We'll be right here if you need anything."

As Barney disappeared into the crowd, I couldn't help but feel a chill run down my spine. Someone had committed this horrible act during our beloved town event. The once-joyful day had taken an unexpected turn, leaving us all reeling in shock and disbelief.

And though I knew I should have been focused on comforting Hazel and Florence, the wheels in my head were already turning, trying to piece together the puzzle that lay before me. Who could have wanted Heidi dead? And more importantly, who would dare to strike during such a public event?

Hazel's face contorted with anger as she stared down at Heidi's lifeless body, her fists clenched at her sides. "That no-good, scheming woman!" she spat, oblivious to the tears streaming down her cheeks. "I knew I should never have trusted her!"

"Easy there, Hazel," I cautioned, stepping forward to place a comforting hand on her arm. "Let's not get too worked up just yet."

"Too worked up?" she scoffed, pulling away from me. "That woman might have cost me the prize, Tilly! She swore she only gave..." Hazel clammed up.

Something else was going on besides a murder. What was Heidi involved with that might have gotten her killed? And how was Hazel involved? I could tell Hazel was on the verge of breaking down, but I couldn't help but wonder if her anger and frustration were also masking something else.

Just then, Felix arrived on the scene, his face a mask of shock and genuine sorrow. "Heidi... no," he whispered, staring at her lifeless form in disbelief.

Barney had returned to stand by Heidi's body, waiting for his deputy to arrive. He sidled up to Florence, attempting to comfort her.

Felix leaned into Uncle Jack and said, "I wonder if she got in too far for her own good."

Intrigued, I stepped closer to Felix. Was this related to what Hazel had previously hinted at?

These questions burned in my mind as the celebratory Parade of Patios turned into a grim march towards uncovering the truth. And as we all stood there amidst the shattered glass and trampled flowers, I couldn't shake the feeling that the killer was still lurking among us.

I couldn't help but notice the tension that filled the air as Felix and Uncle Jack exchanged glances. Unkie, always one to get straight to the point, asked the question on everyone's mind.

"What was going on, Felix?" Uncle Jack's voice was steady, almost devoid of emotion, but I could see the concern in his eyes.

Felix hesitated for a moment before answering. "I suspected something was going on," he admitted, rubbing his chin thoughtfully. "But I never imagined it would lead to... this."

I waited, hoping Felix would continue. This might not be the place to grill him, but I wanted to take advantage of the opportunity.

Right on cue, Felix said, "I knew that Bloom-X was going to be trouble the first time Heidi mentioned it."

"Did anyone else know about this?" I wondered aloud.

Felix shook his head. "Not that I'm aware of. But Heidi had connections all over town. Who knows who else she may have been involved with?"

As we contemplated the implications of Felix's words, Barney stepped forward, his face set in a stern expression. "Alright, everyone," he barked, "We need to secure the scene. This is now a crime scene, and we must treat it as such."

Hazel whimpered as Barney's deputy, Geno, began putting up yellow crime scene tape around her once-pristine garden. The colorful flowers and carefully arranged decorations suddenly seemed less vibrant, tainted by the dark cloud of suspicion that hung heavy over us all.

"Promise me you won't go snooping around, Tilly," Uncle Jack said, noticing my determined expression. "This is a job for the police."

"Of course, Unkie," I replied with a smile, knowing full well that my curiosity wouldn't easily be contained. "Let's give them some space," I said quietly, turning away from Hazel's grief-stricken face and Heidi's lifeless body. We moved toward the street, where a small crowd had gathered, drawn by the commotion and the piercing scream that still echoed in my ears.

"Can you believe this?" Linda whispered, her eyes wide with shock. "Right in the middle of the Parade of Patios!"

"Something isn't right here," I muttered, my mind racing with questions and suspicions. Uncle Jack put a comforting hand on my shoulder, but I could tell that he, too, was deep in thought.

CHAPTER THREE

The scent of freshly squeezed lemons wafted through Luna's Bakery. I scooped generous dollops of luscious cream into our signature cupcakes. The bakery was my sanctuary, the place where I could escape from the chaos of life and find solace in the art of baking.

"Can you believe it, Tilly?" Linda piped up, her voice tinged with a mixture of shock and disbelief. "Heidi, dead? In Hazel's garden, of all places!" She shook her head, her brows furrowed in concern as she continued to zest the lemons.

I sighed, pausing in my task of piping cream onto the golden-brown cupcakes. "It's terrifying, Linda. A killer on the loose, right here in Belle Harbor." My hands trembled slightly at the thought, but I quickly regained composure and resumed my work.

"Did you hear what Felix said?" Linda asked, her eyes wide with curiosity. "Something about Heidi being involved with that illegal Bloom-X growth substance?"

"Yeah," I replied, trying to keep my voice steady. "It makes me wonder if her involvement with Bloom-X had anything to do with her murder." The thought sent shivers down my spine.

Linda nodded, biting her lip nervously. "You think someone might have killed her over some gardening stuff? That's just... insane!"

"Desperate people do desperate things, Linda," I mused, reflecting on the lengths one could go for the sake of winning or keeping something dear.

We continued our morning routine. The unsettling feeling remained, lurking in the corners of the bakery like an unwanted shadow. Heidi was gone, and someone in Belle Harbor had blood on their hands. The question that haunted me most—who could it be?

"Here's my plan," I said, pausing my cupcake assembly line. "I'm going to talk to Felix and the other garden owners near Hazel's house. Maybe they can shed some light on this whole situation."

"Are you sure that's a good idea, Tilly?" Linda asked, her eyes filled with concern. "Whoever killed Heidi might be dangerous, especially if they think someone's snooping around."

"Trust me, I'll be careful," I reassured her. "Besides, I can't just sit here and let a murderer walk free in Belle Harbor. We deserve to know the truth."

With that, I finished preparing the last of the cream-filled cupcakes and left Linda in charge.

I grabbed my backpack and wove my way through the beach cottages.

From the moment I stepped into Grace's garden, it was clear that something extraordinary was happening here. The colors were more vibrant, as if an artist had taken a brush and painted each petal with the most saturated hues imaginable. The size of the blooms was remarkable too—roses the size of teacups, dahlias as big as dinner plates, and sunflowers towering high above my head.

"Amazing," I whispered to myself, feeling as though I'd stumbled into a scene from *Alice in Wonderland*. What could cause such incredible growth?

"Hello, Tilly," Grace called out, appearing from behind a trellis covered in sweet peas, her cheeks flushed from tending to her plants. "What brings you here today?"

"Hi, Grace. I, um... actually wanted to talk to you about Heidi," I said hesitantly, bracing myself for her reaction.

Her face crumpled immediately, and tears welled up in her eyes. "Oh, Heidi," she choked out, dabbing at her cheeks with a well-worn gardening glove. "She was such a good friend, Tilly. I can't believe she's gone."

I reached out and placed a comforting hand on her arm, but I couldn't let my sympathy cloud my judgment. "Grace, I'm trying to find out who could have wanted her dead," I said gently. "Do you have any idea who might have had a motive?"

"Who would want to hurt Heidi?" she sobbed. "She was always so kind and helpful. Even when she was struggling herself, she went out of her way to help others."

"Sometimes people have secrets we don't know about," I suggested delicately, not wanting to upset her further. "Maybe there was something going on in her life that made her a target."

"Secrets?" Grace sniffed, wiping her nose on the back of her glove. "I don't know, Tilly. She was pretty open with me, but... there might have been things she kept to herself."

"Anything you can tell me could help," I urged, hoping she'd confide in me.

Grace hesitated for a moment, as if weighing her options. Then she let out a long sigh and lowered her voice. "There is one thing," she said, her eyes darting around nervously. "But you have to promise not to tell anyone."

How could I make that promise when it might keep me from finding a killer?

"Promise, Tilly. Please," Grace implored, her eyes shimmering with unshed tears.

"Of course, I promise," I assured her, my concern for Heidi's case pushing me to uncover whatever secret Grace was hiding.

Grace took a deep breath, steadying herself. "Alright," she whispered, her voice wavering. "I... I used Bloom-X on my garden."

My eyebrows shot up in surprise. Bloom-X was the illegal growth enhancer Heidi had been involved with. "You did? But why, Grace?"

"Because Heidi asked me to," she admitted, her hands wringing together anxiously. "She told me that if I won the gardening competition, it would really help her out financially. She was struggling, Tilly, as a single mom with a teenage daughter. I just wanted to help her."

My heart ached for both Grace and Heidi. As much as I disapproved of using illicit substances, I couldn't help but feel sympathy for their plight. "So Heidi supplied you with Bloom-X?" I asked, making sure I understood the situation correctly.

"Yes." Grace nodded, a tear finally slipping down her cheek. "But please, Tilly, don't let anyone know about this. I don't want to get into trouble, and I certainly don't want to tarnish Heidi's memory."

"Your secret is safe with me," I promised, though I knew I'd have to weigh my options carefully when it came to sharing this information with others. "Is there anything else you can share with me about Heidi? Anything that might help me find her killer?"

Tears welled up in Grace's eyes, and she looked away before nodding. "There is something else," she admitted, her voice barely more than a whisper. "Owen... Owen and Heidi used to be together."

"Really?" I replied, surprised by this revelation. "I had no idea they were ever in a relationship."

Grace wiped her tears with the back of her hand. "It didn't end well. He found out she was having an affair, and it broke his heart."

"Did Owen ever talk about it? Do you think he could have held a grudge against Heidi?" I asked cautiously, not wanting to upset Grace further.

"No, but I know he was hurt," Grace said, her voice cracking. "I just don't want to believe he could've done something so terrible, Tilly."

"Neither do I," I murmured, trying to process this new information. And then, as if a light bulb flicked on inside my brain, I suddenly saw everything with shocking clarity. "Grace, Hazel's garden! It was absolutely stunning, right?"

"Of course," Grace replied, sniffling. "Everyone knows Hazel had the best garden in town this year. She has a good chance to take the prize."

"Exactly!" I exclaimed, feeling the pieces fall into place. "And if Heidi was supplying Bloom-X to Hazel, and Hazel wouldn't want that information to come out. That means..."

"Blackmail," Grace whispered, her eyes widening in realization. "Heidi could've been blackmailing Hazel to get more money for herself and her daughter."

"Or Hazel could have found out about the other Bloom-X customers and decided to eliminate the competition. With Heidi out of the picture, the supply of Bloom-X might just dry up," I added, my heart racing. "Either way, we have a new lead to follow."

"Please be careful, Tilly," Grace implored, her eyes filled with concern. "The person who did this is still out there, and they might not hesitate to strike again."

I stepped out of Grace's garden, feeling the weight of her revelation heavy on my shoulders. With newfound determination, I set off down the street towards Owen's place.

CHAPTER FOUR

"I hope I can get some answers from Owen," I muttered to myself. My thoughts consumed by the tangled web of relationships and motives surrounding Heidi's death.

As I walked, I couldn't help but notice the beauty of Belle Harbor's gardens, each one striving to outdo the next. It was hard to imagine that beneath their vibrant colors and lush foliage lay a dark undercurrent of deceit and murder. But then again, life often had a way of surprising us—like a cream-filled cupcake hiding an unexpected burst of flavor.

"Alright, Tilly," I whispered to myself, taking a deep breath. "Time to channel your inner detective and get some answers."

With a firm knock on the door, I braced myself for whatever lay ahead. After what felt like an eternity, Owen opened the door, looking disheveled and surprised to see me.

"Tilly?" he muttered.

"Hi, Owen. Do you have a minute?" I asked.

"Uh- sure," he stuttered, his face betraying a mix of confusion and unease. "Why don't you come in?"

"Actually," I replied, glancing around as if the killer might be lurking nearby, "I think it's best we talk outside."

"Alright, then," Owen said hesitantly, stepping out onto his porch. "Let's go back to my garden so we can have some privacy."

I followed him along a path next to his house.

"Your garden is amazing," I replied, returning his smile as I took a few steps closer. "It's like something out of a fairy tale."

"Thanks," he said, a hint of pride creeping into his voice. "I've put a lot of work into it. It's my sanctuary, you know? A place to escape from the world for a while."

"Seems like we all could use a place like that," I mused, my thoughts briefly drifting back to the whirlwind of events that had led me to this point. But now wasn't the time for introspection—I had questions that needed answering.

"Anyway," I continued, clearing my throat as I refocused on the task at hand, "I wanted to talk to you about a few things. Can we take a seat somewhere?"

"Sure thing," Owen replied, gesturing toward a cozy-looking bench nestled beneath a canopy of flowering vines. "Let's sit down and chat." His disheveled clothing with stained t-shirt over sloppy gray sweats stood in stark contrast to the immaculate garden.

"Owen," I began, carefully choosing my words. "Grace told me something... interesting. She said you've been using Bloom-X."

His face paled, and he looked at me with wide eyes. "That's ridiculous," he stammered, shaking his head in disbelief. "I don't know what she's talking about."

"Come on, Owen," I pressed, trying to keep my tone light despite the gravity of the situation. "I'm not here to judge you or anything. But I need to get to the bottom of this whole mess, and I can't do that if people aren't being honest with me."

He glanced away, clenching his jaw as he stared at the vibrant blooms swaying gently in the breeze. "Fine," he muttered after a moment, his voice strained. "Yes, I've used Bloom-X. But it was only once, I swear."

"Thank you for being honest with me," I said, offering him a reassuring smile despite the nagging feeling that there was more to the story. "Why did you use it?"

"Look, Tilly," he sighed, rubbing his temples in frustration. "Hazel's been making my life a living hell ever since she denied my business permit. I thought if I could just hurt her chances of winning the competition, even by just a little, it would level the playing field."

"Except now Heidi is dead," I pointed out gently, watching as his expression crumpled with guilt. "And her friend Grace is mixed up in all of this, too."

"Grace?" he asked, his eyes narrowing with suspicion. "What does she have to do with any of this?"

"According to Grace, she was helping Heidi sell Bloom-X," I explained. "She said it was to help her out financially."

"I had no idea it would come to this," Owen muttered under his breath, running a hand through his greasy hair in frustration.

"I'm sorry," I said somberly, my thoughts drifting to the chaos that had been unleashed on our once-peaceful town.

"Owen," I began cautiously, choosing my words carefully as I broached the subject of his relationship with Heidi. "Can you tell me about your breakup? What happened between the two of you?"

He stared at me for a moment, his eyes flicking away nervously before he responded. "It's... complicated. We had our differences, like any couple, but things got worse when I found out she was cheating on me."

"Cheating?" I echoed, my eyebrows shooting up in surprise. "How did you find out?"

"Does it matter?" he snapped, clearly uncomfortable with the direction the conversation was heading. But I couldn't let it go—not when there was still so much left unsaid.

"Owen," I pressed gently, "every detail is important if we're going to get to the bottom of this. Can you at least tell me if you know who she was involved with?"

He hesitated for a moment, his face contorted with conflicting emotions. Finally, he shook his head. "I never found out the identity of her lover," he admitted, his voice cracking slightly. "And now I'll never get the chance to ask her."

"Owen, why didn't you try to find out who it was?" I asked, genuinely curious.

He sighed, bowing his head. "I wanted to, believe me. But part of me thought that it would just hurt more knowing the truth. I couldn't handle it, Tilly. I loved her, and..." He swallowed hard, avoiding my gaze. "It tore me apart."

His words struck a chord within me, reminding me of my own heartbreak when I discovered my husband's infidelity. As much as I wanted to believe Owen was telling the truth, I couldn't shake the nagging feeling that there was more to his story.

"Owen, I understand how difficult this must be for you," I said softly, placing a hand on his shoulder.

He looked into my eyes, and for a moment, I thought I saw a flicker of fear. But just as quickly, it was gone, replaced by a steely resolve.

I probably got all that I was going to get from Owen for now. "Thank you, Owen."

"Of course," he said, forcing a smile. "I just want this whole mess sorted out as much as you do."

I studied him carefully, noting the way his hands trembled as he spoke and the subtle flush that colored his cheeks. Was he being truthful or hiding something deeper? Only time would tell.

"I promise I'll do my best to find out what really happened to Heidi." I stood and hoisted my backpack over my shoulder.

"Please do," he whispered, his eyes glistening with unshed tears. "She didn't deserve any of this."

With that, I left Owen's garden. Stopping on the sidewalk, I pondered returning to the bakery or continuing my sleuthing with other gardeners. I shot Linda a quick text to see how she was holding the fort down. She replied all good. I smiled. Even if it wasn't, I felt confident she wouldn't say anything. That woman was a treasure. While I was on a roll, I decided to proceed to Mary's house and ask her some questions. Clearly Bloom-X was at the center of this mystery. But did it play into Heidi's death?

CHAPTER FIVE

"Wow," I muttered under my breath, stopping at the gate to Mary's garden to take it all in. This was no ordinary garden; it was a botanical wonderland filled with exotic plants I had only seen in pictures or on television. There were towering elephant ears with leaves as big as beach umbrellas. Delicate orchids were suspended from trellises. And some sort of creeping vine that looked like it belonged in a fairy tale. A small water feature gurgled peacefully near the entrance, flanked by lush ferns and what appeared to be carnivorous pitcher plants.

"Mary really has an eye for this," I thought as I walked up the path towards her front door. It was clear that she wasn't just a casual gardener; this was the work of someone who had studied and honed their craft over many years. No wonder she had won last year's garden prize—this was a masterpiece.

"Hello, Tilly!" Mary called cheerfully, appearing at the doorway just as I reached the top step. She was wiping her hands on a brightly colored apron that matched the garden's exuberance. "What brings you by this morning?"

"Hi, Mary." I smiled, glancing back at the garden before meeting her gaze. "I just wanted to say how absolutely stunning your plants are! I've never seen anything like it. You have a real gift."

"Thank you, Tilly," she replied, beaming with pride. "It's definitely a labor of love, but I wouldn't trade it for anything. Some people collect stamps or knit sweaters. I create my own little wonderland right here in Belle Harbor."

"Did you study horticulture or something?" I asked, unable to hide my admiration. "Your garden is just... incredible."

Mary's eyes lit up, and she nodded enthusiastically. "Yes, actually! I have a degree in horticulture, and I used to work at the agriculture extension office at the local college. That experience really gave me an edge for winning the prize last year."

"Wow, that's amazing," I said, truly impressed by her dedication. I hesitated for a moment before adding, "I hate to say this, Mary, but there are rumors that some gardeners used an illegal product called Bloom-X. Do you know anything about that?"

Mary's eyes widened, and her lips pressed together in a thin line. "Tilly, I'm offended you'd even suggest that. I have the knowledge and experience to care for my plants the right way. I don't need to stoop to using something like Bloom-X."

"Of course, Mary," I blurted, feeling guilty for having upset her. "I didn't mean to imply otherwise. It's just...with everything going on, it's hard to know who to trust."

"Trust?" A flicker of anger remained in her eyes, but after a moment, she sighed and shook her head. "Heidi's death has shaken us all. I can understand why you'd be suspicious, though I'm afraid I don't know how I can help you."

"Any information helps, really." I looked down at my hands as sadness washed over me. "Heidi was so full of life, and now she's gone. I just want to find out who did this to her, you know?"

"I understand," Mary agreed, her voice softening. "I didn't know her very well, but I always appreciated her enthusiasm for gardening, even if we didn't agree on every technique."

"Technique?" I asked, curious.

"Never mind," she said, waving the thought away. "It's not important. What matters is finding justice for Heidi."

"Right," I nodded, trying to shake off the nagging feeling that there was more to what Mary had said than she was letting on.

"Anyway," Mary continued, "if there's anything else you'd like to know about my garden or my experiences with Heidi, feel free to ask. But please, no more insinuations about cheating."

"Agreed," I assured her, feeling both embarrassed and grateful for her understanding. "I promise, no more talk of Bloom-X."

"Good," she said with a smile. "Now, how about a little tour since you didn't get to do that during the Parade of Patios."

As we strolled through the garden pathways, I couldn't help but notice a few unique plants that seemed oddly familiar. There were these gorgeous crimson fire lilies with their delicate petals curled back like tiny flames. And a rare blue moon rose bush whose blossoms were a shade of blue so deep it looked almost purple.

"Mary," I said, my curiosity getting the better of me, "I can't help but notice that some of your plants are quite similar to the ones in Hazel's garden. Is there a reason for that?"

Mary's smile faltered for a moment, and she crossed her arms defensively. "Well, Tilly, I suppose it's not something I like to talk about, but since you've already noticed... I believe Heidi was stealing some of my more unique plants and giving them to Hazel."

"Stealing?" I gasped, shocked at the accusation.

"Yes," Mary explained, her voice tight with frustration. "You see, last year I spent a small fortune on some rare and unusual plants to give my garden that extra edge. When I started noticing that some of my plants had gone missing, I was devastated. And then I saw those very same plants popping up in Hazel's garden."

"Did you ever confront Heidi about it?" I asked, trying to imagine the gentle, gardening-loving Heidi as a plant thief.

"Of course!" Mary said indignantly. "But she denied everything and accused me of being paranoid. I had no proof, so there wasn't much I could do about it. In the end, I had to take out credit to replace the stolen plants. That's why winning the prize this year is so important to me—I need the money to cover my costs."

I frowned, feeling a mix of sympathy and confusion. Could Heidi really have stolen from Mary? And if so, what was her motive? As much as I wanted to believe in Heidi's innocence, it was hard to ignore the evidence that stood before me in Mary's garden.

"Mary, I'm so sorry you had to go through that," I said, reaching out to place a comforting hand on her arm. "No one deserves to have their hard work and dedication undermined like that."

Just as I was about to pose another question to Mary, a tall, muscular man in work clothes approached us. His arms were covered in tattoos, and he had a pair of hedge trimmers in his hand. It was Cole, the tree trimmer.

"Excuse me, Mary," he said, wiping sweat from his brow. "I wanted to double-check with you about trimming that large rhododendron shrub over by the fence. Did you want me to shape it into a sphere or more of a natural look?"

"Ah, Cole, thank you for asking," Mary replied, pausing to consider her options. "Let's go with a natural look this time. I think it'll blend better with the rest of the garden."

"Natural it is," Cole said with a nod, before heading back towards the shrub in question.

Mary turned back to me, her eyes curious. "You mentioned you had a few more questions, Tilly?"

"Right," I said, gathering my thoughts. "Did you know anything about Heidi's relationship with Owen?" I asked, trying to gauge Mary's reaction.

Mary furrowed her brow and shook her head. "Not much, really. I knew they were seeing each other, but beyond that, I didn't pry, unlike some of the other nosy neighbors."

"Did you ever get the sense that Heidi was involved with anyone else?" I probed.

"Other than Owen?" Mary paused, biting her lip. "Honestly, I can't say for certain. Heidi was a private person when it came to her love life."

"Interesting," I murmured, trying to see whether Mary knew more than she was revealing.

"Actually, now that I think about it," Mary began, her voice hesitant, as if she was contemplating whether to share this information with me. "I overheard something odd once. It was when Heidi was last here, just a few days before the tragedy."

"Go on," I encouraged, leaning in closer, my curiosity piqued.

"Well," she continued, casting a nervous glance at Cole, who was now diligently trimming a nearby hydrangea bush. "I overheard Heidi talking intimately with Felix of all people. They were standing just outside my garden gate, and I couldn't help but eavesdrop a little." She blushed slightly, clearly embarrassed by her own nosiness.

"Wait, Felix? As in Hazel's neighbor Felix?" I asked incredulously. The plot was thickening faster than the weeds in my own neglected garden.

"Exactly," Mary confirmed, nodding solemnly. "It seemed quite, umm, passionate. I don't know the details, but it definitely suggested there might have been something more between them."

"Goodness," I muttered, processing this revelation. A potential love triangle involving Owen, Heidi, and Felix was certainly unexpected. And given how high the stakes were in our tight-knit gardening community, it wasn't impossible that such a tangled web of relationships could lead to murder.

"Thanks for sharing that, Mary," I said sincerely, making a mental note to investigate further. "I'm sorry for dredging up memories of Heidi like this, but uncovering the truth is important."

Her eyes clouded with sadness at the mention of Heidi. "I hope you find the answers you're looking for, Tilly."

CHAPTER SIX

As I left Mary's house, the image of Felix and Heidi together played over in my mind like a broken record. Who would've thought that Felix would be tangled up in this mess? It was time to talk to him again, but first, I needed to see my Uncle Jack. He always had a way of helping me find clarity in these situations.

A gentle music played over the loudspeakers along the boardwalk at the beach. At mid-day, the place was filled with families enjoying the sand and sun.

I stopped and looked in Florence's bookstore. Nobody was inside except Florence and her companion cat. She had a duster in her hands, running it over the shelves. She must be beside herself with her sister smack dab in the middle of this murder mystery. Slowing opening the door so I didn't startle her, I quietly said hello.

She whipped her head up, a glassy look in her eyes.

"Just checking in." I said, "How's Hazel doing?"

She raised an eyebrow, clearly a little surprised by my visit. "Hazel? Uh, well, she's been better, I suppose."

I could tell she wasn't expecting me to ask about her sister, but it was the perfect opportunity to gather some information. After all, Hazel had to be one of the prime suspects in Heidi's murder.

"Is everything okay with her? I mean, with all this mess going on, I can't imagine how she must be feeling."

"Of course not," Florence responded defensively, her arms crossing as she looked away. "But you know Hazel. She's strong. She'll get through it."

"Ah, yes," I muttered. "Strong as ever." My mind raced with questions, but I knew I had to tread carefully if I wanted any answers from Florence. "Anyway," I said, brushing a stray strand of hair behind my ear. "I guess we all have our ways of coping, right?"

"Indeed," Florence replied, her gaze returning to the shelf she was dusting. It was clear that she didn't want to discuss Hazel any further, but I couldn't afford to leave without trying.

"I bet she's pretty focused on winning that garden prize. So that's probably keeping her busy," I said. Could I get her talking more about what lengths Hazel might go to in order to win?

Florence chuckled softly, a wry smile creeping onto her face. "Oh, yes. Hazel has always been one for competition, ever since we were children. It's like she has this burning need to prove herself, you know?"

I nodded, aware of the undercurrent of bitterness in her words. I couldn't help but seize the opportunity to dig deeper. "So, do you think Hazel would... stretch the rules to come out on top?" I asked carefully, watching Florence's reaction closely.

Her eyes flicked to my face, then away just as quickly. She fiddled with a small silver locket hanging from her neck, something I had never seen her touch before. "Well," she started hesitantly. "I wouldn't put it past her. Hazel can be... resourceful when she needs to be."

I leaned in slightly, hoping to encourage more from Florence. "Resourceful? Like, bending the rules to get what she wants?" My heart pounded in my chest, the thrill of a possible lead sending a jolt of adrenaline through me.

"Perhaps," Florence murmured, the corner of her mouth tightening as if she had tasted something sour. "But that's just how she is. Always has been."

My mind raced with possibilities, trying to connect the dots between Hazel's competitive nature and her potential involvement in Heidi's murder. Could Hazel have stretched the rules far enough to commit such a heinous act? And if so, why? Tepidly opening the subject, I said, "I bet that made for an interesting time growing up."

Florence hesitated for a moment, her eyes drifting towards the dusty biography section as if searching for answers. "There was an incident back in college... or rather, before we started college."

"Go on," I urged gently, my curiosity piqued, hoping to keep her talking.

"Well, Hazel and I both applied to the same prestigious university," she began, fiddling with the edge of her silk scarf. "I had better grades and more extracurriculars, but somehow, she got in, and I didn't."

"Did you ever find out why?" I asked, trying to keep my tone neutral.

Florence shook her head, a wry smile playing on her lips. "No, but I always suspected she cheated somehow. Maybe she bribed someone, or..." She trailed off, unwilling to voice her suspicions any further.

As I listened to Florence's story, I couldn't help but sense a hint of resentment in her tone. It struck me that this old grudge might be coloring her view of her sister's actions now. If Hazel were willing to cheat to get into college, could she have stooped even lower to win a gardening competition? And what of Heidi's murder?

The door quietly squeaked open, a younger couple entering the bookstore.

I stepped closer to Florence, eager to get any additional details I could before she left to tend to her customers.

"Sometimes I wonder if things would have been different if I'd gotten in instead of her. But there's no point dwelling on the past, is there?"

"No," I agreed softly, grabbing her hand. "But understanding the past can sometimes help us make sense of the present."

Florence glanced at the couple as they browsed the classics section. That was right up Florence's alley. I suspected she was eager to chat with them. I needed to get to the point before I lost her attention.

"Speaking of the present," I said, trying to steer the conversation back on track, "do you know anything about the relationship between Hazel and Heidi? Were they friends or just business acquaintances?"

"From what I've seen, their relationship was strictly professional." Florence hesitated for a moment, her brow furrowed in thought. "Though, I must admit, I don't have any specific details about it."

I eyed her carefully, noting the slight tremble in her voice as she spoke. How far was I willing to push her?

"Would you mind if I asked around town about their relationship?" I ventured cautiously. "Maybe someone else saw something that could help fill in the gaps."

"By all means, ask away." She shifted uneasily, avoiding my gaze. "Just don't be too surprised if you find yourself knee-deep in Belle Harbor gossip."

"Trust me," I grinned, "I've heard it all before. After living here for a while, I'm practically immune to gossip. One more thing before I go."

Florence tilted her head and slightly squinted her eyes.

Shifting gears, I gulped, hoping I didn't tick her off too badly. But I had to know. I clenched my fists. "Have you heard anything about this Bloom-X product that's been making the rounds in town?"

Florence raised an eyebrow, clearly caught off guard by my question. "Bloom-X? Can't say that I have. What is it, some kind of fertilizer?"

"Something like that," I replied, watching her closely for any signs of recognition or deception. "Apparently, Hazel has been using it in her garden, and some people are saying it might not be entirely... above board."

"Really?" Florence feigned surprise, but there was a certain stiffness to her posture that suggested she might know more than she was letting on. "Well, I can assure you, Tilly, I have absolutely no involvement in my sister's gardening endeavors. As you know, I prefer books to plants."

"Well, I better let you help your customers," I said, nodding slowly as I considered the implications of her words. If Florence was telling the truth, then it was possible that Hazel was hiding something from even her own sister.

The moment I was outside, my mind began buzzing like a swarm of bees at a summer picnic. Was Florence's resentment towards Hazel clouding her judgment? The uncertainty gnawed at me, like a pesky itch I couldn't quite reach. If Hazel was as competitive as Florence described, what lengths might she go to for the prize?

CHAPTER SEVEN

The soft tinkle of the bell above the door announced my arrival, and I stepped into Uncle Jack's antique store with a warm smile and a wave. The familiar scent of aged wood and musty old trinkets enveloped me like a comforting hug as I took in the cozy clutter of the shop. Unkie was hunched over a table in the coffee corner, his head close to Barney's. They were deep in conversation, their voices hushed.

"Hey, you two conspirators," I called out, approaching them with a teasing grin. "What are you plotting now?"

"Ah, Tilly, just in time!" Uncle Jack exclaimed, straightening up and beaming at me. His gray hair was tousled, and his glasses had slipped down his nose. "We were just discussing the latest happenings in our peaceful little town."

"Speaking of which," I said, glancing at Barney, who raised an eyebrow and leaned back against the counter. "I wanted to share some information with you guys. I've been talking to the gardeners around town, and I'm starting to think Owen might have more to do with Heidi's murder than we initially thought."

"Really?" Unkie asked, his eyes widening. "What makes you say that?"

"You know how much people love to gossip when they're getting their hands dirty in the soil," I said, rolling my eyes. "Apparently, Owen ended things with Heidi after finding out she was having an affair. And from what I gathered, he didn't take it too well."

"Interesting," Barney mused, rubbing his chin. "We knew about the breakup, but not the reason behind it. This could definitely give Owen a motive."

"Exactly," I agreed, feeling a flutter of excitement in my chest. "And it's not just that. Some of the gardeners hinted that Owen had been acting off recently, like he was hiding something."

"Or maybe he was just upset about the breakup?" Uncle Jack suggested, his brow furrowed in concern.

"Maybe," I conceded. "But I can't shake the feeling that there's more to it than that. Something's not adding up, and I want to find out what."

"Of course you do," Barney said with a sigh, though there was an affectionate glint in his eyes. "Just be careful, Tilly. We don't want you getting hurt."

"This could be the break we've been looking for," I continued, my voice rising with excitement. "If Owen really had a reason to want Heidi dead—"

"Slow down, Tilly," Barney interjected, raising a hand to halt my rapid-fire deductions. "You've given us some useful information, but let's not jump to conclusions just yet." He glanced at Uncle Jack, who nodded in agreement.

"Right, we need to let the police do their job," Unkie said gently, giving me a reassuring smile. "But we appreciate you keeping your ears open." He always cautioned me about getting involved, knowing full well I couldn't help myself.

"Speaking of ears..." I hesitated, my enthusiasm waning as I remembered the worried expression on Florence's face during my visit with her. "Florence seems really concerned about Hazel's potential arrest."

Unkie's brow furrowed, and I could see the worry etched in the lines around his eyes. "I haven't had a chance to speak with her today, but it's understandable that she'd be worried. Hazel is her sister, after all."

"True," Barney conceded, scratching his head. "I reassured her as much as I could this morning. But we have to follow the evidence, no matter where it leads. I'm doing everything I can to clear Hazel's name, if she's innocent."

"Mmm hmmm," I mumbled, not wanting to imply any criticism of Barney's work. "It's just...Florence looked so stressed. Can you imagine what it would feel like if someone you loved was accused of murder?" I slapped my hand over my mouth, realizing I had been in this exact situation previously with Uncle Jack. My eyes teared up, remembering the stress we felt when he had been wrongly accused and jailed for the murder of Linda's former boyfriend. I thought my world had ended with his arrest, and I vowed to leave no stone unturned to exonerate him. Thankfully, here we were today with his innocence and freedom.

"That's in the past," Unkie stepped forward, draping an arm around my shoulder and squeezing.

I stuttered a breath as he released me, the memory quickly fading to focus on the present.

I hesitated a moment before plunging ahead. "Do you know anything about Felix? You know, the neighbor who suspected Heidi of providing illegal plant growth material to Hazel?"

"Ah, Felix," Uncle Jack mused, scratching his head as if trying to recall every interaction he'd had with the man. "He's come into the shop a few times looking for garden decorations. Seemed like a nice enough guy, always polite and friendly."

"Really?" I asked, my curiosity piqued. "Well, I heard something interesting today that might be worth mentioning."

Unkie raised an eyebrow, waiting for me to continue. As I hesitated, debating whether to share the juicy piece of gossip I'd picked up, I could see the anticipation in his eyes.

"Alright, fine," I relented with a sigh, knowing that Uncle Jack or Barney would pry it out of me, eventually. "I heard that Felix might've been having an affair with Heidi. Owen said he thought she was cheating. But he didn't know with who."

"Whoa," Uncle Jack said, his brows shooting upward in surprise. A playful smile tugged at the corners of his mouth, though, as if he couldn't help but be amused by the whole tangled mess. "That certainly puts a new spin on things, doesn't it?"

"Definitely. I guess you never really know what goes on behind closed doors," I said, feeling a twinge of excitement despite myself.

"Isn't that the truth?" Barney chimed in, leaning against a polished mahogany armoire. He looked thoughtful for a moment before adding, "I haven't heard anything about Felix and Heidi's supposed affair. But it's definitely something I'll be looking into. Thanks for the tip, Tilly."

"Anything to help, Barney," I replied with a grin. My mind was already racing ahead, trying to fit this new piece of information into the larger puzzle of Heidi's murder.

"Alright, Tilly," Uncle Jack said, as his warm gaze lingered on me with concern. "I know you've got that sleuthing instinct of yours, but promise me you'll be careful and not take any unnecessary risks." He gestured toward Barney, who nodded in agreement. "Let our good friend here handle the case—that's his job, after all."

I glanced between the two of them, their faces filled with worry for my safety. It was touching to have people care so much, but at the same time, a little frustrating. I wanted to help solve this mystery, and I felt like I was onto something.

"Okay, okay," I relented, holding up my hands in surrender. I stepped forward and hugged Uncle Jack, immensely grateful for our relationship. He had become a surrogate father for me after I had moved to Belle Harbor. Not wanting to do anything to damage that relationship, I promised myself to be as careful as I could. "Love you, Unkie." I turned and left the two of them to continue their conversation.

As I headed to my car, my phone buzzed in my pocket. Expecting to see a text from Justin about meeting at my house for dinner, I stopped in my tracks. An unknown number was calling.

CHAPTER EIGHT

"Hello?" I answered hesitantly, curious.

"Is this Tilly?" The voice on the other end was distorted, almost unrecognizable.

"Who's asking?" I replied, my grip tightening around the phone.

"Someone who knows what you've been up to and has a piece of information you might find interesting."

I furrowed my brow, my heart skipping a beat. "If you have something to say, just say it."

"Alright." The mysterious caller paused for dramatic effect, making me roll my eyes despite the situation. "Not only did Owen use Bloom-X, but he's been buying it under a fake name for months."

"Wait, what?" I stammered, feeling a mix of surprise and doubt. "How do you know this?"

"Let's just say I have my sources," they replied cryptically. "And if I were you, I'd start digging a little deeper into Owen's past. You might be surprised by what you find."

Before I had a chance to respond, the line went dead, leaving me standing there with a buzzing phone pressed against my ear and a heavy knot of uncertainty settling in my chest. If Owen had been using Bloom-X for months under a fake name, it meant he had more to hide than just trying to out-do Hazel's garden.

I lifted my head up and glanced around. The families, who earlier in the day had populated the beach, had disappeared, likely headed to dinner. How did this call play into the investigation? I needed to get home and diagram this all out. The tangled web had become quite complicated.

The moment I stepped inside my cozy little cottage, a wave of relief washed over me. It had been an exhausting day of poking and prodding into other people's lives. My feet were killing me, and all I wanted was to settle in for a quiet evening.

"Is that you, Tilly?" Justin's voice echoed from the kitchen, accompanied by the mouthwatering aroma of garlic and tomato sauce. I tossed my keys onto the entry table and kicked off my shoes, instantly feeling the tension in my shoulders ease.

"Yep, it's me," I called back, padding toward the kitchen, where I found him unpacking takeout containers filled with Italian goodness. "Oh, thank heavens for pasta," I sighed, wrapping my arms around him for a quick hug. "You're a lifesaver."

"Anything for my favorite amateur sleuth," he teased, planting a kiss on my forehead before returning to the task at hand. He set out plates and silverware, along with the food. I couldn't help but feel grateful for the sense of normalcy he brought to my life amidst the chaos and intrigue that seemed to follow me wherever I went.

"Looks like you've had quite the day," he commented, as he handed me a steaming plate of spaghetti marinara. "I figured this might bring some comfort after all your investigating."

"Comfort food is precisely what I need right now," I admitted, gratefully accepting the dish. We carried our plates to the dining room table and settled in to eat, the warm glow of the overhead light casting a welcoming ambiance over the familiar scene.

"Everything okay?" Justin asked, snapping me out of my reverie. "You look a bit jumpy."

"Sorry, it's just been a long day," I replied, trying to shake off the stress.

"Don't forget to take care of yourself," Justin encouraged, reaching out to give my hand a quick squeeze.

I wiggled my toes beneath the table to ease my aching feet. Yes, this was exactly what I needed—a brief respite from amateur sleuthing, surrounded by the warmth and familiarity of home.

"Did you remember the garlic knots?" I asked with a teasing grin.

Justin grabbed the bag and opened it toward me. "Of course," he replied, rolling his eyes playfully. "You know I'd never forget your favorite."

"Good man," I praised him, plucking one of the knots from its bag and biting into it with gusto.

"Alright," I said between bites, "I've got some updates for you about my little investigation today." Justin raised an eyebrow, giving me his undivided attention. "First off, Grace. She's been helping Heidi sell Bloom-X to make some extra cash, but she seemed genuinely upset about her friend's death. I'm not convinced she had any motive to kill her."

"Interesting," Justin mused, taking a bite of his spaghetti. "And what about Owen?"

"Ah, Owen," I sighed, twirling a forkful of noodles. "He admitted that he had ended things with Heidi after finding out she was having an affair. He seemed genuinely hurt by it all."

"An affair?" Justin said, eyebrows raised. "With whom?"

"Here's where it gets juicy," I said, pausing for dramatic effect. "Felix, another gardener vying for the garden prize. And speaking of prizes, Mary was the winner last year, and she might be feeling threatened by Hazel as her competition. So, both Felix and Mary could have motives too."

"Wait, so you're saying that Owen knew about the affair?" Justin asked, leaning forward with genuine concern.

"Exactly. But he claims he broke up with Heidi once he found out. But it's hard to say if it was enough to push him over the edge," I replied, taking a sip of my wine to wash down the last bite of garlic bread. "He claimed he didn't know who she was cheating with."

"Sounds like it's time for you to get out the pen and paper and draw your infamous spider chart," Justin suggested.

I chuckled. Infamous. The diagram always helped me to organize my thoughts. And sometimes it highlighted things my brain just couldn't connect until I saw them in black and white.

"Actually, that's not a bad idea," I agreed, impressed by his suggestion. We both got up from the table and cleared our plates, making room for a large sheet of paper and a pen. I couldn't help but smile at the small domestic scene we had created.

I drew a circle in the middle of the paper and wrote Heidi's name inside. I drew spokes out from the hub, one for each of our suspects.

"Okay, let's start with Grace," I said as I wrote her name at the end of one line. "Suspected motive: jealousy over Heidi's success in the gardening community." I shook my head, feeling like she was low on the list.

"Right. And then there's Owen," Justin continued, watching me intently as I added Owen's name to the chart. "He knew about the affair, and he was hurt by it."

I sat back in my chair, rubbing my temples, unsure if this was helping or not. Maybe getting this out of my head might allow it to percolate on the back burner while I slept. I could only hope.

"Let's not forget Felix and Mary," Justin added, reminding me of their potential involvement. I added them to our evolving picture.

"Justin, do you think we're on the right track here?" I asked, biting my lip nervously as I glanced up at him.

"I think we should keep a neutral perspective until we get this completed." He tapped the paper.

"And then there's Hazel," I continued, adding her name to the chart. "Town council president, Florence's sister, and the woman desperately trying to win the garden prize. She wanted—no, need-ed—Heidi's illegal substances to make her garden the best in town."

I connected Hazel's name to the motive we'd just discussed. "But what about the others? Did Hazel know about the other buyers? And did any of them have a reason to want Heidi dead?"

My head spun with questions, and I could feel anxiety creeping in, threatening to overwhelm me. I hesitated, my pen hovering over the chart as I considered whether to share the information I'd received earlier in the day.

"Tilly?" Justin jolted me out of my trance.

"Before I came home," I began slowly, "I got an anonymous phone call."

"Anonymous?" Justin's eyebrows shot up in surprise. "What did they say?"

"According to the caller, Owen's been buying Bloom-X under a fake name," I admitted, biting my lip as I watched him process the information. "I don't know what to make of it, though. Is it significant? Or just someone trying to throw me off track?"

Justin leaned back in his chair, clearly deep in thought. "That's a tough one. Did the caller have a distinct voice or anything that could give us a clue about who they are?"

I shook my head, frustrated by my inability to provide any concrete details. "Nothing stood out to me. It was just... a voice. I couldn't tell if it was male or female, young or old. It might as well have been a robot, for all the help it gives us."

"Still," Justin said, tapping his fingers on the table as his mind raced, "it's a lead. And right now, we need all the leads we can get. If Owen really was buying Bloom-X, could that be a connection between him and Heidi's murder?"

"Maybe," I said, though doubt still lingered in the pit of my stomach. "But it's such a tenuous link. I don't want to jump to conclusions without more evidence."

"Right," Justin chimed in, grabbing a garlic knot. "And Owen ended his relationship with Heidi after discovering the affair, so he clearly didn't take it well."

"Exactly," I said, leaning over the table to scribble down some notes beside Owen's name. "So, let's say he found out about the Bloom-X and confronted her about it. Things could have escalated from there, and... well, you know."

We both stared at the chart before us, the lines connecting the various suspects and their motives crisscrossing like a spider's web.

"Based on everything we know so far, Owen seems like the most likely suspect," I concluded, tapping my finger against his name on the chart.

"Agreed," Justin said, folding his arms and studying the chart intently.

I stood, grabbing the empty containers. We had decimated the contents and my stomach felt heavy. I was certain the answer was right in front of us, hiding in plain sight. Was it really Owen?

CHAPTER NINE

"Morning, Mrs. Thompson! The usual?" I called out, sliding a steaming mug of dark roast towards an elderly woman who smiled appreciatively. With a practiced flick of my wrist, I filled a plate with her favorite raspberry scone and handed it over.

"Thank you, dear," she said, shuffling towards her usual corner table. "You always know just what I want."

"Happy to help!" I replied cheerfully, turning back to the growing line of eager faces waiting for their breakfast fix. I took immense pride in knowing the regulars' orders by heart. It made me feel connected to this little community of Belle Harbor, which had welcomed me with open arms after my disastrous marriage ended.

"Two iced coffees and a cinnamon roll, coming right up," I announced, springing into action.

As the morning rush began to wane, the bakery's cacophony of voices and laughter gradually subsided. It was replaced by the soothing hum of the espresso machine and the soft clink of cutlery on plates.

"Phew, finally, a chance to breathe," I muttered to myself, wiping sweat from my brow as I surveyed the nearly empty café. Just then, Hazel walked in, her face etched with worry.

"Hey, Hazel," I greeted her, trying to lighten the mood. "What can I get you? Maybe a scone and some tea to calm those nerves?"

"Uh, sure, Tilly," she replied hesitantly, her eyes darting around the bakery. "Just a chamomile tea, please."

"Coming right up," I said with a wink, preparing her order as Hazel found a table by the window.

"Here you go, enjoy!" I followed her to the table and handed her the steaming cup. She thanked me with a weak smile.

I couldn't imagine the weight on her shoulders, Heidi dying at her home. Was she truly innocent, or was her world about to be turned upside down?

The last few customers trickled out, leaving only Hazel and me in the once-lively café.

I leaned against the counter, taking a moment to rest my tired feet as I stole glances at Hazel. She seemed unusually fidgety, constantly checking her phone and tapping her fingers on the table.

Her phone buzzed to life, startling both of us. She answered it with a hasty, "Hello?"

I wondered if everything was OK over there, my curiosity piqued. Though I tried to appear nonchalant, replenishing the supply of pastries in the display case, my ears strained to pick up snippets of her conversation.

"Wha- what do you mean?" Hazel hissed into the phone, her voice cracking with tension.

"Uh-huh... No, I can't talk about this here." She glanced around nervously, her eyes landing on me. I quickly focused on the tray in front of me, trying not to look suspicious.

"Look," she continued, lowering her voice to a barely audible whisper, "I don't know anything about the murder."

My pulse quickened, adrenaline coursing through my veins. A shiver of fear danced down my spine. The word *murder* hung in the air like a shadowy specter, refusing to be ignored.

"Alright, fine." Hazel sighed, rubbing her temples as if to ward off a headache. "But if anyone asks, I was just dealing with some council business."

"Jack's niece runs this place, you know," she added cautiously, never taking her eyes off me. I could feel her gaze boring into my skull, but I kept my head down, pretending to be engrossed in my work.

"Okay, bye." Hazel hung up, her hands shaking ever so slightly. She took a deep breath, attempting to regain her composure.

"Is everything alright, Hazel?" I asked innocently, feigning ignorance. "You seem a bit on edge."

"Err, yes. Fine, just... business matters," she stammered, avoiding eye contact. "You know how it is."

"Of course," I replied, unable to shake the nagging feeling that Hazel was hiding something far more sinister than council business.

I watched as she finished her tea, her eyes darting around the room as if searching for an escape route.

"Business matters, huh?" I asked, raising an eyebrow and leaning against the counter. I tried to sound casual, but my racing heart betrayed my true intentions. "You know, Hazel, I'm a pretty good problem solver. If something's bothering you, I'd love to help."

Hazel's eyes widened in surprise, her hands fidgeting with the napkin on the table. She forced a smile, but it came out more like a wince. "Really, Tilly, it's nothing you need to worry about. Just some boring council stuff."

"Sure didn't sound like 'boring council stuff' from what I heard," I pressed, refusing to back down. A memory of Aunt Marge's words echoed in my head: "Curiosity killed the cat, but satisfaction brought it back." Well, this cat wasn't going anywhere until she got some answers.

"Look, Tilly," Hazel said, her voice strained and her face flushing red. She shifted uncomfortably in her seat. "I appreciate your concern, but it's really not any of your business."

"Isn't it?" I challenged, crossing my arms. "We're talking about a murder here, Hazel. The whole town is on edge, and if there's something you know that could help clear things up, don't you think it's important to share?"

"Murder?" Hazel scoffed, her eyes darting around nervously. "I never mentioned anything about a murder. You must have misheard me."

"Come on, Hazel," I countered, feeling a surge of determination. "I heard you loud and clear. Let's just cut to the chase, alright? What were you and the person on the phone talking about? Maybe it could help clear your name."

"Alright," she whispered, barely audible over the hum of the display case. "It was Cole. I spoke to Cole, the tree trimmer."

"Go on," I encouraged gently.

"Fine," she exhaled, glancing nervously towards the door. "He was the one who helped me dispose of the branches after trimming the trees around my yard. The whole thing was... more complicated than expected."

"Complicated? How so?" I prodded, unable to shake the feeling that there was still something significant hidden beneath her words.

"Because... because we had to get rid of them discreetly, without attracting attention," Hazel admitted, her voice wavering. "We didn't want anyone from the garden committee seeing the mess and docking points from my score."

"Is that all?" I asked, raising a skeptical eyebrow. It seemed innocent enough, but my gut was telling me there was more to the story.

"Yes!" Hazel insisted, her face flushed with frustration. "That's all there is to it, Tilly. Nothing more." She jammed her papers into her bag and stood, waving her arm as she exited the bakery without another word.

"Okay." I sighed, deciding not to push her further for now.

I watched Hazel's retreating figure, her posture tense as she left the bakery. The door swung shut behind her, its bell jingling softly in the suddenly quiet space.

"Did I push too hard?" I wondered aloud, rubbing my temples. I paced back and forth behind the counter, trying to piece together the fragments of information I had just been given. There had to be a connection somewhere, but what was it?

"Trees...branches...garden prize," I muttered, the words tumbling out like puzzle pieces waiting to be assembled. My mind raced, entertaining every possible scenario. "Could it really be just about the garden competition?" I sighed, frustrated by the lack of clarity.

"Hey Tilly, are you okay?" Linda asked, catching me off-guard as she emerged from the kitchen, wiping her hands on her apron.

"Well," I began hesitantly, shifting my weight from one foot to the other, "Hazel claims she was just talking to Cole about disposing tree branches. But something about it just doesn't feel right."

"Interesting," Linda mused, her brow furrowing in thought. "What do you think is really going on?"

"I don't know yet," I admitted, my face scrunching up in determination. I grabbed a towel and mindlessly wiped down the tables in the lobby. Maybe getting my hands back into some dough might distract me enough for the pieces of the puzzle to form a coherent picture.

CHAPTER TEN

The sweet scent of honeysuckle greeted me when I arrived at Unkie and Linda's charming Victorian home. My limbs ached from another long day at the bakery, but anticipation bubbled inside me like an uncorked bottle of champagne. I pushed open the garden gate and stepped onto the cobblestone path leading to their back patio, my heart racing with each step closer to the truth.

"...and then she said, 'I swear it's haunted!'" Uncle Jack guffawed, throwing his head back as he recounted a story to Linda and Barney. They were gathered around a wrought-iron table adorned with a vase of fresh flowers, the laughter and chatter washing away any lingering tension. The murder investigation seemed a world away in this moment, and for that, I was grateful.

"Ah, Tilly, there you are!" Linda beamed, rising from her chair to greet me. Her warm embrace felt like coming home, and I couldn't help but smile.

"Long day, kiddo?" Uncle Jack asked, his eyes twinkling with concern and pride.

"Exhausting," I admitted, sinking into an empty seat. "But worth it."

"Here, have a glass of wine," Linda suggested, pouring a generous helping into a delicate crystal goblet.

"Thanks." I took a sip, savoring the rich, velvety taste as it soothed my frayed nerves. I closed my eyes and slipped down into the cushiony patio chair. "Keep going with your story. I really need some comic relief."

"Well, she insisted that the antique mirror she bought from my shop had a ghost living in it," Unkie continued, chuckling. "She claimed it whispered secrets about her neighbors at night!"

"Goodness!" Linda gasped, while Barney snorted with laughter. I couldn't help but join in, our combined mirth filling the air like music.

As we laughed, I noticed something out of place—a pair of shears lying on a nearby table. They looked eerily similar to the ones used to kill Heidi, and my heart skipped a beat. Trying to appear nonchalant, I picked them up, running my fingers over their sharp edges.

"Where did these come from?" I asked, struggling to keep my voice steady.

"Those? Oh, they're just a spare pair we have for trimming the hedges," Linda explained, her brow furrowing with confusion. "Why do you ask?"

"Nothing, they just reminded me of... something." I hesitated, knowing that mentioning the murder would only bring worry back into their lives.

"Actually," Linda said, "those shears were custom made by Cole, the tree trimmer. He makes them for anyone who needs a sturdy pair for their gardening. They're the best pair we've ever had."

My ears perked up at the mention of Cole's name. "Really?" I asked casually, trying not to betray my sudden interest. "That's fascinating."

"Indeed. He's quite skilled with metalwork," Uncle Jack added, nodding his approval.

"Speaking of skilled individuals," I said, seizing the opportunity to share my suspicions. "I've been thinking a lot about Heidi's murder, and I'm starting to believe that Felix or Owen might have had the strongest motive to kill her."

"Go on," Barney prompted, leaning forward in his chair.

"Owen was in a relationship with Heidi, but he ended things after discovering her affair. Though at the time, he didn't know it was with

Felix. And Felix, as you know, is Hazel's neighbor." My mind raced as I connected the dots, adrenaline coursing through my body.

"You're right," Unkie said, retrieving the shears from me, turning them over in his hands.

"Oh, yeah!" I said, pulling out a folded sheet of paper from my backpack. "Justin and I spent last night going over everything we know about the suspects, and we came up with this chart." I spread the paper across the table, revealing our color-coded web of connections and motives.

"Wow, Tilly, this is quite impressive," Barney remarked, leaning in to study the chart. Uncle Jack and Linda also moved closer, their eyes scanning the intricate lines that linked the names of Felix, Owen, and other potential suspects.

"Thank you," I replied, feeling a mix of pride and trepidation.

Uncle Jack quietly asked, "And what about Hazel?" He followed the line that connected her name to the others. "She's mentioned here, but her motive seems less clear."

"True," Barney said, "But we can't rule her out yet since the murder occurred at her house."

As we continued discussing the chart, I noticed Uncle Jack studying me closely. His perceptive eyes seemed to pierce through my carefully composed façade, as if he could sense the storm of emotions roiling beneath the surface.

"Something's bothering you, Tilly," he said gently, his voice laced with concern. "You've been on edge ever since you arrived. What's going on?"

I hesitated, torn between the desire to unburden myself and the fear of revealing too much. But as I looked into Jack's compassionate eyes, I knew I could trust him with my secrets.

"Alright," I sighed. I told him about the anonymous phone call I had received the previous night. "The caller gave me a clue, which could help us solve the crime," I divulged, my heart pounding as their eyes widened with surprise.

Barney scratched his beard, still not entirely convinced. "Tilly, we've seen it before. Sometimes people are fantastic at pretending. We can't be sure about their intentions. It could be someone trying to throw us off track."

"Or even worse, lure you into a dangerous situation," Uncle Jack added, his brow furrowing with concern.

"What else did they say? Could you tell who it was? Was it a man or woman? Was—?" Barney fell right into his investigative mode.

I held my hand up. "I couldn't tell anything about who it might be. They just said we should dig into Owen's past." Glancing at Barney, I nodded. "You're probably already doing that, aren't you?"

He chuckled. "We're pretty good at our job, Tilly."

Relieved, I hoped I could let some of this go. The stress was getting to me. I held out my empty glass to Linda, who jumped up to refill it.

"Barney, how is Florence holding up?" I asked. "I can't imagine how difficult it must be for her to deal with all this suspicion and scrutiny on her sister."

"Unfortunately, Tilly, she's not faring too well," Barney sighed, running a hand through his thinning hair. "Florence is convinced that Hazel might be arrested for the murder since it happened at her house. She's been trying to keep her sister calm, but Florence has been on edge ever since."

"Is there anything we can do to help?" I asked, determined to ease even a little of my friend's suffering.

"Let's focus on finding the truth, Tilly," Uncle Jack said firmly, echoing my earlier resolve. "That's the best way we can support Florence and everyone else involved in this mess."

We sat quietly, letting the gravity of the situation weigh upon us. With all resources geared toward this investigation, I was certain

Barney would prevail in finding Heidi's killer? But would it happen before there was another victim?

CHAPTER ELEVEN

I started my little VW bug, ready to head home and fall into bed for a good night's sleep. I shifted into gear to begin the brief trip, lost in thought from my conversation about Heidi's killer. Rambling down the side streets to my little cottage, Cole's house loomed ahead, an unassuming abode nestled amongst its neighbors. Barney's warning echoed in my head, urging me to stay out of the investigation.

"Really, Tilly," I muttered under my breath. "You've got a business to run. And don't forget about that wedding you're planning." My fingers fidgeted with the engagement ring on my finger.

Cole was one of the people I hadn't talked to yet. As he was in the gardening business, perhaps he had some insight into some of the suspects that might help clarify which of them could have killed Heidi.

Pulling into his driveway, I immediately noticed something odd: the door to his barn was slightly ajar.

"Okay, Tilly," I muttered under my breath, "you can do this." My hands gripped the steering wheel tightly, my knuckles turning white. Despite my best efforts, my thoughts were racing a mile a minute. What if Cole caught me snooping around? What if there was nothing to find? Would he think I was just being nosy?

"Focus, girl!" I chided myself. This was about Heidi, not me or my bruised ego. With a determined nod, I climbed out of the car and slowly approached the barn.

Each step felt like walking on eggshells as I tried to be as quiet as possible. The gravel crunched beneath my feet, betraying my presence to anyone who might be listening. I reached the barn door and hesitated for a moment, taking a deep breath before carefully peering inside.

An icy shiver ran down my spine, and I couldn't shake the feeling that someone was watching me. I tried to focus on the task at hand, but the nagging sensation persisted. "Maybe it's just Cole," I thought, trying to reassure myself. "He probably wants to know what the heck I'm doing snooping around his barn."

"Alright, Tilly, time to face the music," I whispered under my breath, steeling myself for a potentially awkward confrontation.

"Hey, Cole, I was just—" My words were cut off as I suddenly found myself pushed violently to the ground. The wind was knocked out of me, and I gasped for air, trying to make sense of what had just happened.

"Stay out of this, Tilly!" a muffled voice growled down at me. My vision swam, but I could make out a dark figure looming above me, their face obscured by a mask. Panic set in, my heart hammering in my chest as I realized this wasn't Cole.

"Wh-who are you?" I stammered, my voice barely audible. "What do you want?"

"Didn't you hear me? Stay out of the investigation, or it won't end well for you!" The masked assailant's voice was cold and threatening, leaving no room for negotiation.

"Please, I... I won't do anything, I promise," I choked out, tears streaming down my face. All thoughts of playing amateur sleuth had vanished, replaced by sheer terror.

"Good." The figure seemed satisfied with my response, but there was a note of warning in their tone. "Don't forget: I'm watching you. One wrong move, and you're done."

With that, the masked stranger disappeared into the darkness, leaving me trembling on the ground, my entire world turned upside down.

I lay on the ground, my heart pounding like a runaway train as I tried to process the situation. The masked assailant had vanished as quickly as they'd appeared, leaving me alone in the darkness next to Cole's barn. I took a few deep breaths, attempting to steady my nerves and focus on what had just happened.

"Okay, Tilly," I whispered to myself, "you're not hurt, just scared. Let's get out of here."

With shaky legs, I pushed myself up off the ground and made my way back to my car. The gravel crunched beneath my feet. I couldn't help but look over my shoulder every few seconds, half expecting the masked figure to reappear at any moment.

"Focus, Tilly," I muttered under my breath, trying to quell the fear that threatened to overwhelm me. "Just get home and regroup. You can do this."

Once inside the safety of my car, I locked the doors and finally allowed myself to release the breath I didn't even realize I was holding. My hands were trembling, so I gripped the steering wheel tightly to steady them before starting the engine.

"Home, sweet home," I mused, forcing a weak laugh. "I never thought I'd be so grateful to see my driveway."

"Time to regroup and rethink," I declared, unlocking the door and stepping inside. "Because whoever you are, masked menace, you've messed with the wrong baker."

"Could that call I received earlier have been from the masked assailant?" I wondered aloud, my suspicions mounting as I recalled the voice that taunted me over the phone. "What if they're watching me?"

My hands trembled as I mentally replayed the chilling encounter with the elusive figure. The air inside felt heavy, and a shiver ran down my spine.

With a deep breath, I stepped into the living room, only to notice something strange on the floor. A folded piece of paper lay just beneath the door, as if someone had slipped it under while I was out.

"Great, more surprises," I grumbled, bending down to pick up the mysterious note. My heart raced as I unfolded the paper, unsure of what to expect. The words scribbled across it sent a cold wave through my body:

"LOOK INTO FELIX—HE MAY BE THE ONE YOU SEEK."

"Who left this?" I asked the empty room, knowing no answer would come. "Is this a genuine tip or a ploy to throw me off track?"

I dropped my backpack on the kitchen table and started the tea kettle in desperate need of something to soothe my nerves. I headed to the bedroom to change into pajamas.

I sat on the edge of my bed, clutching the note in my shaking hands. The paper trembled as if it were a living thing, reflecting the whirlwind of emotions that surged through me. Felix, Hazel's neighbor? The same man who was having an affair with Heidi behind Owen's back? Could he really be her killer?

I took a deep breath and forced myself to think logically.

Heidi, the victim, had been supplying illegal substances to several people in town, including Felix. She needed the money for her teenage daughter, but what about Felix? What did he have to gain from all this, apart from a secret tryst with the woman who provided him with those substances?

"Maybe he wanted more than just an affair," I pondered aloud. "Maybe he wanted control over the supply, or maybe he just wanted to keep his secrets hidden."

The tea kettle screamed from the kitchen, jolting me from my trance. I prepared some chamomile tea and grabbed the chart from my backpack, opening it on the table. Adding the new information since initially creating the diagram, I hoped to see the picture better. I needed a follow-up with Felix to confirm my suspicions. But it had to be a public place. Could I get Uncle Jack to request Felix to meet him at the antique shop under the guise of showing him a new piece that had arrived that might be perfect for Felix's garden? My gut told me

we were getting closer to solving this murder.

CHAPTER TWELVE

I jolted awake, my heart pounding like a jackhammer in my chest. The remnants of a nightmare clung to me like cobwebs, but they were quickly pushed aside by the very real anxiety swirling through my mind. Recent events had taken their toll, leaving me sleepless and on edge.

"Ugh," I muttered, rubbing my temples as if that would somehow ease the pressure building inside my skull. Glancing at the clock, I realized it was still early, but there was no chance of getting back to sleep now. With a sigh, I reached for my phone on the nightstand and scrolled through my contacts. It was time to get some answers.

"Barney," I whispered to myself, tapping his name and pulling up our text conversation. My thumbs hovered over the screen, hesitating for a moment before I began typing. "Meet me at Jack's shop ASAP. We need to talk."

I quickly pulled up Linda's contact info, letting her know I would be late to start the baking for the day. With all of this sleuthing, I might need to hire someone else at the bakery to help out.

I hastily pulled on my clothes and grabbed my backpack, pausing to look at the note that had mysteriously arrived the night before. Was I getting in too deep?

Jumping in my car, I sped toward the beachfront. Unkie normally arrived early to his antique shop, getting a pot of coffee started for the visitors that would arrive throughout the day. I only hoped he would be there when I arrived.

"Barney?" I called out, my voice sounding meeker than I intended. "You here?"

"Back here, Tilly," his gruff voice responded from the shadows near the rear of the shop. As I made my way toward him, navigating through aisles lined with teetering stacks of books and curious trinkets.

The smell of fresh-brewed coffee wafted toward me.

"Thanks for meeting me here, Barney," I began, fiddling with the hem of my shirt.

Unkie handed me a steaming cup of coffee and beckoned me to one of the nearby chairs.

"OK. What have you got?" Barney asked, leaning against an ancient-looking armoire with folded arms. His impatience only fueled my anxiety.

"Okay, okay." I took a deep breath and pulled a crumpled envelope from my pocket. "I got this note yesterday. No return address, just my name hastily scrawled across the front." I handed him the note, trying my best to ignore the tremble in my hand. "Read it for yourself."

As Barney unfolded the paper, I chewed at my lip, watching his expression shift from confusion to concern. I knew I wasn't overreacting—there was something truly sinister about those words.

Unkie leaned toward Barney, reading the note.

Barney scrutinized the letter, his eyes narrowing as he studied the handwriting. He glanced up at me with a puzzled expression. "This looks eerily familiar, Tilly. I just can't put my finger on who it reminds me of..."

"Really?" My heart raced at the prospect of a lead, even if it was only a vague one. "Do you think it could be someone we know?"

"Maybe," he muttered, still poring over the scrawl. I shifted weight from one foot to another, trying to curb my impatience.

I glanced around the antique shop, my gaze lingering on a vintage mirror that had seen better days. It was tarnished and slightly cracked, but it still held a certain charm—much like the rest of Jack's collection. As I turned back to Barney, an idea began to form in my mind.

"Barney, have you considered Felix as a suspect?" I asked, my voice barely above a whisper, remembering his connection to Heidi and Hazel. "He's been acting strangely ever since that whole Bloom-X fiasco."

"True," Barney agreed, stroking his chin thoughtfully.

"Wait a second," I blurted, my thoughts racing as an idea struck me like a bolt of lightning. "What about Sylvia?"

"Who?" Barney asked, momentarily thrown off by the abrupt change in topic.

"Sylvia," I repeated, my voice rising with urgency. "I heard she was selling Bloom-X to Cole, but didn't use it herself. We haven't talked to her yet, have we? She could be our key to understanding what's going on!"

Uncle Jack and Barney shared a meaningful look, and I could tell that there was something they weren't telling me. My curiosity piqued, I folded my arms across my chest and raised an eyebrow expectantly.

"Alright, you two," I said firmly, my tone brooking no argument. "Spill it. What's going on with Sylvia?"

Barney sighed, realizing that I wouldn't let the matter drop until I had answers. He glanced at Uncle Jack one last time before turning back to me, his expression serious.

"Okay, Tilly, here's the deal," he began, his voice low and conspiratorial. "We've been monitoring Sylvia ever since we found out that she was selling the Bloom-X product. We need to see if she's connected to Felix and this whole mess somehow."

"So, what's the plan? How are we going to get Sylvia to talk?"

"Actually," Barney said, "we've got something in the works already. A little sting operation, if you will."

My heart skipped a beat at the mention of a sting operation. This was it—our chance to finally get some answers and put an end to this nightmare once and for all. I could hardly contain my excitement as I turned to face them both, determination burning in my chest.

"Count me in," I declared, my voice unwavering. "Whatever it takes to solve this case, I want to be a part of it."

But as I looked into Barney's eyes, I could tell that he had reservations about involving me in the plan. And as the silence stretched on, I realized with a sinking feeling that I might not convince him otherwise.

"Come on, Barney," I pleaded, my voice taking on a slight whine. "I've been in the thick of this from the start. You can't just leave me out now."

Barney sighed, rubbing his temples as if trying to ward off an impending headache. "Tilly, you're not a cop. This is a delicate operation, and I can't risk your safety."

"Delicate?" I scoffed, crossing my arms over my chest. "We're dealing with murder here. Delicate left town a long time ago."

A tense silence fell between us as we stared each other down, both unwilling to budge. I could practically hear the gears turning in Barney's head as he weighed his options. Finally, Uncle Jack cleared his throat, breaking the standoff.

"Look, Barney," he said, placing a reassuring hand on his friend's shoulder. "You've seen what Tilly can do when she sets her mind to something. She's resourceful and determined. Maybe having her there isn't such a bad idea."

"Exactly!" I chimed in, nodding vigorously. "I can be an asset, Barney. I promise."

He shook his head. "I just can't chance it. I'll be sure to report back to you when we're done."

I softened my tone for one last attempt. "How about this? I stay in the car. I'll just watch from there."

Barney glanced at Uncle Jack who shrugged his shoulders. I could practically hear the resolve cracking.

"But you promise you'll stay out of the way." Barney jabbed his finger toward me.

I leaped at him, gripping him in a bear hug. I hoped with all my might this was soon to be over.

CHAPTER THIRTEEN

The rural location we'd chosen for the sting was straight out of a crime thriller. An old, abandoned barn surrounded by overgrown fields that stretched as far as the eye could see. It was the perfect place for a clandestine meeting, far from the prying eyes of Belle Harbor residents.

Barney parked our unmarked car down the street, out of sight but close enough for us to keep an eye on the proceedings. The tension in the air was palpable; it felt like even the wind held its breath, waiting for something to happen. As we settled into our stakeout, with only the soft hum of the car engine for company, I couldn't help but feel a strange mix of excitement and dread.

Just as the tension in the air seemed unbearable, Detective Geno leaned into our car for any last-minute instructions from Barney. The overalls and straw hat were a far cry from his usual uniform, and I couldn't help but chuckle at the sight of him.

"Y'all ready for this?" he drawled, tipping his hat to us with a wink. It was clear that Geno was embracing his role wholeheartedly, and I appreciated the levity it brought to our mission.

"Remember," Barney said, his voice serious again, "you're the buyer here, so act natural. Don't let Sylvia get suspicious."

"Got it, chief," Geno replied, giving us a thumbs up as he hopped in his car and headed toward the barn.

"Here we go," I murmured, gripping the binoculars like a lifeline.

Through the binoculars, I saw Geno strike up a conversation with Sylvia, who seemed cautious but not overly suspicious. Their voices came through the wire we'd planted on Geno, and I listened intently as they discussed the illegal substances.

"Seems like you've got quite the green thumb," Geno said, feigning interest in her gardening expertise.

"Green thumb, huh?" Sylvia replied, a hint of a smile playing at the corners of her mouth. "I guess you could say that."

"Good," I thought, my heart racing with anticipation. "This is going better than I expected."

As their conversation continued, I couldn't help but be impressed by Geno's undercover skills. He asked all the right questions without pushing too hard, never once arousing suspicion. Barney and I exchanged an approving glance.

"Alright, then," Sylvia said at last, her eyes darting around nervously. "Let's get down to business."

"Perfect," Barney whispered, his hand tightening around the radio transmitter. "Just a little more, and we'll have everything we need."

Geno replied, playing along. "Heard it works wonders for plants."

"More than wonders," Sylvia boasted, a sly grin forming on her lips. "One dose of this stuff will have your garden blooming like you wouldn't believe."

"Sounds too good to be true," Geno mused, scratching his chin thoughtfully. "But I reckon I'd like to give it a try." His farmer persona was on full display.

"Great," Sylvia said, her voice barely concealing her relief. "I've got plenty in stock."

Is that so? I thought, my heart pounding with excitement. This was the break we needed—the evidence that would lead us closer to the actual killer.

"Let's see it then," Geno suggested, motioning for Sylvia to show him the goods.

"Alright," she agreed, opening the truck's tailgate to reveal several sacks of the mysterious fertilizer. "This is the real deal, I promise you."

"Let's hope so," Geno replied, examining the bags closely. "My plants are going to love it."

"If this works, there's more where it came from," Sylvia assured him.

"Right," Geno said, shooting a glance in our direction.

"Are we getting anything good?" I asked Barney.

"Maybe." He lifted the binoculars to his face. "We've got Sylvia for selling the stuff on the black market. But ideally we'd get more about how it might have related to Heidi's murder."

"If Heidi had double-crossed someone, maybe they had gotten revenge?" I asked, unsure now that this sting operation would prove fruitful.

Meanwhile, Geno and Sylvia continued their discussion, oblivious to our growing realization that we were barking up the wrong tree. As they hammered out the details of pricing and quantity, I could see the frustration building on Geno's face as well. He glanced at us again, a knowing look in his eyes.

"Alright," Sylvia said, clearly eager to wrap up the deal. "I think we're all set, then."

"Actually," Geno interrupted, desperation creeping into his voice. "Before we close this deal, I was wondering if there's anything else you might have for sale. Anything a bit more... potent?"

Sylvia hesitated before she finally replied. "Well, there is one thing. But I only sell it to a select few customers. It's not exactly legal, either."

"Go on," Geno urged, sensing that we might be onto something after all. Bloom-X looked to be a distraction. There was something else playing into the mix.

"Alright," Sylvia conceded, her voice barely audible. "I've been getting supplies from a guy named Cole. He's got some powerful stuff—way beyond your average fertilizer and this milder Bloom-X. But like I said, it's not exactly on the up-and-up."

My heart raced, and I exchanged a glance with Barney. This was it—the lead we'd been hoping for. Cole. We couldn't be certain of his involvement yet, or if it was a promising connection. He hadn't been anywhere on my radar until now.

"Interesting," Geno replied casually, trying to conceal his own excitement. "Maybe we could do business in the future."

"Sure," Sylvia agreed, visibly relieved that the conversation had shifted away from her own illegal activities. "Just give me a call if you're interested."

"Will do," Geno said.

Sylvia hauled out three bags of what I assumed was Bloom-X. She and Geno exchanged those for cash. Sheila jumped in her truck, speeding from the barn, spewing gravel everywhere as she sped away.

"Did you hear that, Barney?" I whispered excitedly, gripping the binoculars.

"Sure did," Barney replied, his eyes narrowing in thought. "Cole, huh? This might be our ticket to finding out who's really behind Heidi's murder." He stepped out of the car as he pulled out his phone to make a call.

Geno pulled up beside us in the old car, jumping out and dusting off his old overalls. He certainly had a future as an undercover agent, or an actor. Sylvia had played right into his hands. I suspect it worked even better given his charming demeanor.

"Good work," I said to Geno's widening grin.

"Yeah, I hope so." He leaned into the window as Barney returned to the car.

"This might just be the missing piece to our puzzle," Barney said, holding out his phone. "Cole has flown under the radar, but I think we've outed him."

Clapping my hands, I said, "Let's go."

Barney vigorously shook his head. "Not this time. It's getting more dangerous. Only official law enforcement personnel from here on out."

I laced my fingers together in front of me and pleaded, "Please. You have to admit, I behaved myself during this undercover operation. I feel like I need to see this through to the end."

Barney grimaced, as I knew I had won him over. He glared at Geno. "Can she stay with you while we visit Cole?"

"Oh, thank you, Barney!"

He started the car.

"Tilly, we don't know Cole's exact involvement, so you have to be careful. If anything happens to you on my watch, your uncle will have my head." If Cole was dealing something even more powerful than Bloom-X, was it worth killing over?

True. Uncle Jack was quite the papa bear. Never having kids of his own, he had always taken extra care of me. And now that I had moved to Belle Harbor, he was like a second father.

Shifting into gear, we set off for our next stop.

CHAPTER FOURTEEN

"Alright," Barney said, taking a deep breath. "We're here to find out if Cole had any involvement in Heidi's murder. Remember, Tilly, stick to the plan and stay in the car."

"Of course, Chief," I replied, giving him a reassuring smile. But deep down, I knew I couldn't just sit idly by while we were so close to uncovering the truth. And he knew it, too. This was our little dance.

Geno pulled up behind us and met Barney at his car door. They started toward Cole's front door, their footsteps crunching the gravel on Cole's driveway. My heart pounded so hard I felt like I could hardly contain it in my chest. I berated myself for not cluing into Cole earlier. Sometimes it was the person in the shadows that stood out the most.

Cole answered the door, a smile quickly turning to a grimace. Was that a sign of guilt? Barney gently began with an innocuous statement that they were talking to everyone in the gardening community. He asked for Cole's help. Shifting to an amenable posture, Cole said, "Sure."

I couldn't help but feel an overwhelming urge to explore the barn on Cole's property. The towering structure, with its weathered wood and slightly ajar door, seemed to call out to me. As quietly as I could, I opened the car door and took a step toward it, my heart pounding in anticipation.

I approached the entrance, the thrill of defying Barney's orders mixed with the very real possibility of uncovering the truth about Heidi's murder. I pushed the barn door open, wincing as it creaked loudly, and stepped inside.

"Here goes nothing," I whispered to myself, my eyes adjusting to the dim light as I began my search for evidence.

The dim light filtered through the dusty windows, casting eerie shadows that danced along the walls of the barn. I tiptoed further into the space, my eyes scanning the cluttered shelves and old equipment for anything out of place.

As I sifted through the contents of the barn, my fingers brushed against something cold and metallic. Curiosity piqued, I pulled it from the shelf—a custom set of shears, eerily similar to the ones at

Hazel's. My breath caught in my throat. This might be nothing, since Cole created these for his customers.

My gaze landed on a stack of containers shoved in a corner, partially obscured by a tarp. My pulse quickened as I recognized the label: Bloom-X. The illegal substance that had been linked to Heidi's murder. But was there more?

I could hear voices mumbling. Hopefully, they could keep Cole talking long enough for me to find something incriminating. I spotted a tarp along the back wall covering something. Could this be it? I quickly lifted one corner of it to reveal several bags with the label GroXcel. This must have been what Sylvia mentioned. If this was stronger than even Bloom-X, it had to be more dangerous and expensive, too. Was this all about money?

With newfound determination, I hurried back toward the others, doing my best to hide my excitement. As I approached, I heard Cole's voice rising in anger.

"Look, I don't know anything about Felix and Heidi! What do you want from me?" he demanded, glaring at Barney and Geno.

"Easy, Cole," Barney said smoothly, his eyes locking onto mine as I rejoined the group. "We're just trying to get to the bottom of this."

Not wanting to derail Barney's questioning, I hesitated for a second to reveal my discovery in the barn. We were so close to answers I didn't want to jeopardize the investigation.

Barney looked at me, as if to grant permission to speak. Charging full steam ahead, "Alright, Cole," I said, my voice steady despite my racing heart. "What about your little side business with Bloom-X?" I held off on my discovery of the GroXcel for now, planning to bring that hammer down soon.

"Wh-what are you talking about?" Cole stammered, his eyes narrowing with suspicion.

"Cut the act, Cole," I snapped. "I found containers of Bloom-X and those fancy shears of yours in your barn. You know—the ones just like the ones found at Hazel's place? So, care to explain?"

Cole looked as though I had slapped him across the face. His cheeks flushed red, and for a moment, he seemed lost for words.

"Fine, you caught me," he finally spat, gritting his teeth. "So I've got some Bloom-X. Big deal. It's not like it's illegal or anything."

"Actually, it is," Barney interjected, his tone matter-of-fact. "And we all know that you're not using it for any legitimate purpose."

"Look, I don't have to explain myself to you people," Cole shot back, his anger mounting. "And even if I was using it for something other than gardening, what does that have to do with Heidi?"

"How about the GroXcel?" I blurted, hoping to throw him off kilter. "What are you doing with that?"

Cole shifted his weight between his feet and looked at his watch. "Look, I—"

"We're not done yet. We can either finish here or you can come down to the station," Barney said.

"I haven't done anything wrong," Cole pleaded, his voice bordering on a whine.

Goosebumps raised on my arms, certain we were near a conclusion.

Barney continued pressing Cole about his relationship with Heidi. With almost a whisper, Barney said, "Were you upset with Heidi?"

Cole pursed his lips and paused so long I didn't think he was going to answer.

He spat, "Heidi was a pathetic woman who couldn't keep her hands off other men. She left me for Owen. And Felix? He doesn't give a damn about anyone but himself."

"Sounds like you're pretty familiar with their relationship," I observed, watching Cole closely for any signs of deception.

"Doesn't take a genius to see what was going on," Cole shot back, his cheeks flushing red with anger. "For all I know, there was even more than Owen and Felix. They all deserved each other."

I tilted my head to one side as I studied him. "That's an interesting choice of words. It almost sounds like you're harboring some resentment towards them."

"Resentment?" Cole scoffed, his fingers curling into fists at his sides. "You don't know what you're talking about, lady."

"Alright, let's cut to the chase," Barney began, his expression solemn. "We have reason to believe you were at Hazel's house just before Heidi was found dead."

"Excuse me?" Cole scoffed, clearly taken aback by the accusation. But I noticed a flicker of unease flash across his eyes.

"Is it true, Cole?" I asked, my voice barely containing the bubbling mix of suspicion and determination churning inside me.

"Fine," he muttered, looking away for a moment before meeting our gaze once more. "I was there, but I was just removing some brush from Hazel's garden to prepare for the Parade of Patios. It's not like I was doing anything wrong."

Barney's eyes narrowed as he scrutinized Cole, making it clear that he wasn't buying the story. I watched as the tension between them grew, thickening the air like the fog that often rolled in off the harbor.

"Removing brush, you say?" Barney asked, his voice dripping with skepticism. "Funny thing, I spoke to Hazel earlier. She didn't mention any brush needing removal."

"Maybe she forgot," Cole retorted, his voice strained and defensive. His gaze flicked between Barney and me, a nervous bead of sweat forming on his brow. He was starting to crack under the pressure. "You know how she skirts the rules sometimes."

"Or maybe you're lying," Barney shot back. "If you were there for something innocent, why didn't you tell us right away? Why hide the fact that you were at Hazel's?"

Cole stepped back from the porch into the house and quickly tried to slam the door in our face. Geno lunged forward, shoving his foot inside just far enough to keep an opening.

"Get off my property," Cole yelled, and sprinted away from the door.

Geno followed on his heels, grabbing Cole's arm as he picked up a pair of shears from a nearby table. Geno spun Cole around, squeezing his wrist so the shears fell to the floor, cuffing him and reading him his rights.

"Stay here, Tilly," Barney said, following Geno inside.

Nope, I said to myself, right behind him.

"You'll be sorry for sticking your nose where it didn't belong," Cole said to me.

"Are you threatening her?" Barney said as Geno escorted Cole from the house.

Cole dragged his feet, requiring Geno to force him towards the car.

"You might not want to add more charges to the list," Barney said. With Heidi's murder, you're going away for a long time."

"You'll never make it stick," Cole yelled as Geno shoved him into the backseat of his car and slammed the door.

Cole's mouth continued to move. I suspect pleading his innocence. My stomach churned from the encounter.

"One of the oldest motives in the book," Barney said. "Passion gone awry. I'm just sorry for Heidi and her family that it got this far."

"He didn't really confess," I said, getting into the passenger seat of Barney's car. "How can you be so sure of his arrest?"

"Along with Hazel, I talked to Felix earlier today." The old car rumbled to life. "Felix provided all the details about his relationship with Heidi. He mentioned Cole had been in Hazel's yard earlier that day."

"Oh boy," I said. "Felix may not have wanted to tarnish Heidi's reputation. But he probably didn't realize the crucial clue he had by sighting Cole at Hazel's." Whew. I blew out my breath. These investigations could turn on a dime with just the smallest detail.

CHAPTER FIFTEEN

The Parade of Patios was in full swing. Everyone seemed grateful that we could resume the event that had been suddenly halted by Heidi's murder. Cole continued to deny his guilt, but I knew the diligence of the police force would see this through to a satisfying conclusion.

"This is so cool," Justin said, grabbing my hand as we left Mary's yard. He inhaled deeply, taking in the wonderful smells of the many flowers. I wondered if Mary would make it two in a row, however her alleged use of Bloom-X might just keep her out of the running.

We headed to the last stop before arriving at the awards ceremony. Sylvia's. The extent of her role in this garden mystery appeared to be only selling and not using the Bloom-X. Would that disqualify her from the award?

Her garden was an enchanting oasis—a perfect balance of bright blossoms and lush greenery. Two particularly striking features caught my attention. A whimsical, hand-painted gazebo at the center of the garden, adorned with vividly hued flowers. And a row of exquisite topiaries shaped like enchanted creatures from fairy tales. It was clear that Sylvia had poured her heart and soul into her creation.

"Wow!" I marveled, unable to tear my eyes away from the stunning scene before me.

Justin reached for my hand and squeezed. I was so lucky to have him to enjoy these life adventures. We circled Sylvia's garden and turned left down the street to the podium where the award would be announced. The judges had a monumental task in choosing the winner. Even the gardens without Bloom-X were award-winning in my book.

The gardeners and the crowd gathered around as we waited for the announcement. Third place was announced as Felix. I glanced over at him as he half-smiled with a small wave of his hand. Heidi's death must be weighing heavily on him. The second place winner was Kate Sullivan. Her darling little sanctuary included an extensive array of herbs and spices. She organized them so that you could visit a section and harvest them for a specific meal. I especially liked the spaghetti section with the powerful aroma of thyme and basil.

The crowd erupted into thunderous applause as Sylvia's name was called for first place. She beamed with pride as she accepted her well-deserved award. The announcer handed her a shimmering miniature sunflower that sparkled under the sunlight.

"Thank you all so much," Sylvia said, her voice filled with genuine gratitude. "I'm honored to receive this award, and I want to extend my heartfelt congratulations to all the other participants. Your gardens are all truly beautiful, and they've brought so much joy to our community today."

The applause for Sylvia subsided, and she took the opportunity to make an announcement. "There's something else I'd like to say," she said, her voice clear and steady. "I know that Heidi's daughter, Lily, has been struggling since her mother's passing. As a token of my appreciation for all that Heidi did for our community, and in recognition of Lily's bright future, I'd like to donate a portion of my prize money to help start a college fund for her."

The crowd erupted into fresh applause, touched by Sylvia's generosity.

As the award ceremony came to a close, Justin and I made our way over to Hazel's. She had chosen not to attend the ceremony, certain with her use of Bloom-X that she wouldn't win. And I suspected she was embarrassed as the town council president to have stooped to such means just to win.

"Welcome, everyone!" Hazel called out warmly, wiping her hands on her apron. "Please, make yourselves at home." We joined Barney and Florence on Hazel's patio. It was too bad she had cheated, as she really had an eye for garden design. I hoped she could redeem herself for next year's event.

"Did you see the whimsical gnome village in Grace's garden?" Florence asked, her voice filled with delight.

"Or the incredible water feature Owen had installed?" Barney chimed in, clearly impressed by the creativity on display throughout the event.

A cool breeze rustled through the leaves overhead, carrying the sweet scent of blooming flowers.

Hazel returned with a large glass bowl filled with ladyfinger cookies, lemon, and cream. A re-do of the dessert the day Heidi was murdered. It was a work of art. She dished us up each a heaping plateful.

"Did you see how intricate Sylvia's topiary was?" Justin asked between bites of the scrumptious lemon treat. "It must have taken her ages to perfect those shapes."

"Absolutely," Florence agreed, her eyes twinkling with admiration. "And what about the magnificent koi pond in Janet's backyard? It was so serene and calming."

"Indeed," Barney chimed in, his voice filled with awe. "I could've sat there for hours just watching those majestic fish glide through the water."

As our conversation continued, I noticed Hazel gazing thoughtfully at her own garden, a subtle smile playing on her lips. Curiosity piqued, I turned to her and asked, "What are you thinking, Hazel?"

"Seeing all the passion and creativity on display today has inspired me," she replied, her eyes sparkling with determination. "Next year, I want to enter the competition, but not just for the sake of winning. I want to create a garden that truly reflects who I am and what I value. One that brings joy not only to myself but to everyone who visits it."

"Bravo!" Florence exclaimed, clapping her hands to support her sister's newfound ambition. "I know your garden will be absolutely stunning, Hazel."

"Thank you, dear sister," Hazel replied, her cheeks flushed with gratitude.

"Alright," Florence suddenly announced, her voice cutting through the momentary silence like a knife. Her eyes darted around, finally settling on me. "I've been meaning to tell you this, Tilly. I... was the one who wrote that letter to you."

"Wait, what?" I exclaimed, taken aback by her sudden confession. My heart raced in my chest, and I felt a strange mix of shock and curiosity. "Why would you do that?"

Florence shifted uncomfortably in her seat before explaining, "I knew you were close to getting to the bottom of all this mess. I wanted to ensure that my sister was cleared of any suspicion—not only for her sake, but for the town's. Hazel is such an asset to this community, and I couldn't bear the thought of losing her."

"Thank you, Florence," I said, touched by her faith in me. "But you could have just asked for my help instead of sending an anonymous letter."

"I know, I know," she admitted, her cheeks turning a light shade of pink. "But I didn't want to put you in an awkward position or make it seem like I was trying to interfere with Barney's investigation."

"Speaking of which," Hazel chimed in, her voice trembling slightly. "It's still hard for me to process that Heidi was murdered in my yard, by Cole, of all people." She sighed heavily, a look of sadness crossing her face. "If only I had seen him there earlier, maybe I could've stopped him somehow."

Barney, ever the pragmatic one, shook his head softly. "Hazel, you can't blame yourself for what happened. There's no way you could've known what was going to happen. And even if you had seen Cole, confronting him might have put you in danger, too."

"Barney, how did you figure out Cole made that phone call to me?" I asked.

He pointed at me and said, "Good old-fashioned police work. We took what we had to start with. The caller said Owen was buying the stuff."

"I don't get it," I said, confused.

"With the threat of being accused of murder, Owen was happy to plead to a lesser offense of buying illegal goods."

Justin stood and served himself another helping of the trifle. "How does that implicate Cole?"

I chuckled. "Maybe I need to pull out my chart again."

"Turns out Cole made the call, hoping to throw Owen under suspicion," Barney clarified.

"Whoa," I blew out a breath. This investigation work was intense. I shivered at the fact that the killer had called me. How close was I to real danger?

"The list of crimes resulting from this investigation is quite long. Starting with Cole and Steve Hanson as the mastermind behind the illegal substances. Turns out he had been making a pretty penny and had quite a network of sellers."

"Oh," I slapped my hand over my mouth, tears forming in the corner of my eye. "Was that...?"

Barney nodded. "Steve was the person who assaulted you. Cole outed you to Steve, and he started following you."

I didn't realize until now how close to the danger I had been. Maybe it was getting time to hang up my sleuthing. With a wedding soon and my bustling bakery business, I had all I could handle.

"Nothing like job security," Barney said.

Hazel blushed. "I've learned my lesson," she said, holding up her hands in surrender. "I'm grateful that those of us who used Bloom-X only got a fine and community service."

"Here's to new beginnings," I proposed, raising my coffee cup in a toast.

The group seemed to breathe a collective sigh of relief as we moved on from the somber topic.

"Speaking of new beginnings," Hazel said, her eyes twinkling with excitement, "Tilly, Justin, have you two given any thought to your wedding plans?"

"Um, well," I stammered, glancing over at Justin, whose cheeks had taken on a rosy hue. "We've been so caught up in everything lately, we haven't really had a chance to discuss it."

"Ah, I thought as much," Hazel replied, nodding sagely. "Well, in that case, may I make a suggestion?"

"Of course," Justin chimed in, leaning forward with interest.

"Since you both seem to have such an appreciation for beautiful gardens," she gestured around the yard at the incredible beauty, "why not consider having your wedding right here in my garden?"

I exchanged a glance with Justin, who appeared just as surprised and touched by the offer as I was. My mind immediately conjured images of our closest friends and family gathered amid the lush greenery and vibrant flowers. It was a picture-perfect scene that filled my heart with warmth and anticipation.

"Are you sure, Hazel?" I asked hesitantly, not wanting to impose. "It's such a generous offer."

"Absolutely!" she enthused, her face beaming with sincerity. "It would be an honor to have your wedding take place in my garden. And besides, it'll give me the perfect motivation to make sure it's in tip-top shape for the competition next year."

"Thank you, Hazel," I said, my voice thick with emotion. "We would be honored to have our wedding in your garden."

Justin leaned over and kissed me. Soon we would be husband and wife.

ABOUT THE AUTHOR

Sue Hollowell is a wife and empty nester with a lot of mom left over. Finding a lot of time on her hands, and as a lover of mystery novels, she began telling the story of a character who appeared in her head. And she hasn't looked back. She likes cake, and the more frosting the better!